S0-ARG-982

Little
Meerkat's
BIG PANIC

by the same author

Kit Kitten and the Topsy-Turvy Feelings
A Story About Parents Who Aren't Always Able to Care
Jane Evans
Illustrated by Izzy Bean
ISBN 978 1 84905 602 1
eISBN 978 1 78450 064 1

How Are You Feeling Today Baby Bear?
Exploring Big Feelings After Living in a Stormy Home
Jane Evans
Illustrated by Laurence Jackson
ISBN 978 1 84905 424 9
eISBN 978 0 85700 793 3

of related interest

Frankie's Foibles
A story about a boy who worries
Kath Grimshaw
ISBN 978 1 84905 695 3
eISBN 978 1 78450 210 2

The Boy Who Built a Wall Around Himself
Ali Redford
Illustrated by Kara Simpson
ISBN 978 1 84905 683 0
eISBN 978 1 78450 200 3

A Journey in the Moon Balloon
When Images Speak Louder than Words
Joan Drescher
Illustrated by Joan Drescher
ISBN 978 1 84905 730 1
eISBN 978 1 78450 100 6

Little Meerkat's
BIG PANIC

A Story About Learning
New Ways to Feel Calm

Jane Evans

Illustrated by Izzy Bean

Jessica Kingsley *Publishers*
London and Philadelphia

First published in 2016
by Jessica Kingsley Publishers
73 Collier Street
London N1 9BE, UK
and
400 Market Street, Suite 400
Philadelphia, PA 19106, USA

www.jkp.com

Copyright © Jane Evans 2016
Illustration copyright © Izzy Bean 2016

All rights reserved. No part of this publication may be reproduced in any material form (including photocopying or storing it in any medium by electronic means and whether or not transiently or incidentally to some other use of this publication) without the written permission of the copyright owner except in accordance with the provisions of the Copyright, Designs and Patents Act 1988 or under the terms of a licence issued by the Copyright Licensing Agency Ltd, Saffron House, 6–10 Kirby Street, London EC1N 8TS. Applications for the copyright owner's written permission to reproduce any part of this publication should be addressed to the publisher.

Warning: The doing of an unauthorised act in relation to a copyright work may result in both a civil claim for damages and criminal prosecution.

Library of Congress Cataloging in Publication Data
A CIP catalog record for this book is available from the Library of Congress

British Library Cataloguing in Publication Data
A CIP catalogue record for this book is available from the British Library

ISBN 978 1 78592 703 4
eISBN 978 1 78450 246 1

Printed and bound in China

Dear Child,

This story is for you, although you might find the grown-ups want to read it with you (or to have a peek at it when you are not there), so they can understand it too! It is all about three animals who end up working together to solve a problem, but it is also the story of how your brain works and how sometimes it can get scared and anxious and needs help to feel calm again.

I hope that you enjoy the story of Little Meerkat, Small Elephant and Mini Monkey, and that it helps you to understand your brain better so you can learn to spot which part you are using and how that feels for you.

All my best wishes,
Jane

Once upon a time there was a Little Meerkat with a very important job to do. Little Meerkat had been learning how to do this job for such a long time, by watching the other Meerkats and practising over and over again.

Today was the day that it was finally Little Meerkat's turn to be the Lookout Meerkat and watch over the whole Meerkat gang.

Now, if you have ever seen a group of Meerkats you will know that being the Lookout Meerkat is about being wide awake and alert to keep everyone safe from any other animals, snakes or big birds that might come and hurt them.

The very first thing Little Meerkat had to work out how to do was to balance on the Lookout's branch while looking, listening and sniffing, and being ready to taste and feel if anything bad or scary was nearby.

Little Meerkat needed to be ready to sound the alarm by shouting, 'Danger, danger, danger!'

How do you think this made Little Meerkat feel?

important   worried

excited

scared   tired

Little Meerkat had been waiting for this day to come, as it was an important part of becoming a grown-up Meerkat, but now that it was here it all felt a bit too much!

Little Meerkat's neck and shoulders felt tight and hard and both legs were wobbly. Little Meerkat's heart kept jumping about and even breathing felt too fast and difficult to do. Little Meerkat started panting.

Still, it was time! So Little Meerkat tried hard to concentrate, to stop wriggling or fidgeting too much and to keep focused on searching for any danger.

How about you? What does your body do if you feel scared or worried about something?

wobbly   tight

sick

dizzy   something else

Meanwhile, all of the other Meerkats played, chattered, lay around in the sun and chased bugs. After all, with Little Meerkat on watch it was their time to relax.

If there was any danger, Little Meerkat would be sure to sound the alarm so they could get ready to fight, run away, be very still, or go and check it out.

On this bright sunny day Little Meerkat was doing a great job of checking for danger, but soon got tired and sleepy…and it wasn't long before Little Meerkat was sound asleep.

After a short while, Little Meerkat woke up with a jump and immediately started checking to see if everyone was still safe. Imagine how Little Meerkat felt when it turned out that all of the other Meerkats were nowhere to be seen…

Do you think Little Meerkat was feeling…?

confused   frightened

lonely   something else

'Oh no, oh no!' Little Meerkat ran around searching everywhere – under logs, down in the burrows, behind bushes – all with a racing heart and dry mouth, and unable to think at all!

Just then, Small Elephant came wandering by. Little Meerkat rushed up to Small Elephant and tried to find the words to ask for help. But a scared Little Meerkat finds talking tricky, so it all came out in a muddle: 'Sleep me, log, all gone, gone.'

Small Elephant could see that Little Meerkat was struggling to speak and was full of feelings and very hot and bothered.

Small Elephant did not know about being a Lookout Meerkat who had lost all the other Meerkats, but Small Elephant did know how to **imagine** what Little Meerkat might be feeling.

Small Elephant could remember once not hearing Big Poppa Elephant say it was time to leave the water hole.

Small Elephant had been left all alone and felt scared, sad and worried until Big Poppa Elephant came back into sight. Only then did Small Elephant feel safe, relaxed and calm again. So now Small Elephant was able to work that Little Meerkat might be feeling like this about losing the other Meerkats.

In fact, Small Elephant could feel and imagine Little Meerkat's feelings so well that it wasn't long before they were both rushing about looking worried, searching everywhere and bumping into each other!

Just then, Mini Monkey swung down from a tree to see what all the fuss was about. Little Meerkat and Small Elephant were in such a panic that they found it hard to be still and calm enough to explain, and in the end they both burst into tears!

Mini Monkey looked at them and knew what they needed was to feel a bit calmer. Mini Monkey began to gently hum and move from side to side, and then stood and took three big breaths:

Slowly in...and slowly out...

Slowly in...slowly out...

Slowly in...slowly out...

While counting 1234 slowly in...12345678 slowly out...

Little Meerkat and Small Elephant began to calm down. Mini Monkey gently hummed some more and helped them to join in with some counting and big breaths of their own:

1234 slowly in...

12345678 slowly out...

After that, Mini Monkey looked kindly at the worn out, worried Meerkat and Elephant and asked how they were feeling.

> What do you think Little Meerkat and Small Elephant told Mini Monkey about how they were feeling?

For a while the three of them sat near each other, and then slowly Little Meerkat started to tell the story of the missing Meerkats.

Mini Monkey did some thinking, asked some questions, did some planning and suggested they have a cool drink from the water hole before looking for the Meerkats again.

Everyone agreed that this was a good idea.

Mini Monkey suggested they go back to where the gang of Meerkats had first been playing, chatting and lying in the sun. Just as they arrived, Little Meerkat spotted a big rock in the distance and remembered something very important.

Small Elephant could feel that Little Meerkat was getting excited and soon joined in with the pointing and jumping up and down.

Once again, Little Meerkat struggled to say anything, but Mini Monkey quickly did some more thinking and worked out what Little Meerkat was trying to say. 'Aha! I think there is something behind the rock that Little Meerkat is excited about.'

All together the three animals headed for the rock. Mini Monkey suggested that they should quietly and carefully peep behind it.

Imagine their surprise when, right there, they found all the other Meerkats!

Little Meerkat hadn't seen the Meerkats rush to hide behind the rock after they spotted a big bird flying above them towards the water hole.

Of course! The rock had always been the Meerkat's safe place to hide when danger was around, but because of Little Meerkat's big panic about losing all the other Meerkats it had been impossible for Little Meerkat to think clearly and remember this.

From that day, Little Meerkat, Small Elephant and Mini Monkey became very good friends. They worked out that they each had something special to offer the other.

> Can you guess what it was?

Little Meerkat was good at spotting possible danger and sounding the alarm.

Small Elephant was good at working out and remembering the feelings of others.

Mini Monkey was great at thinking, planning, and calming others down.

Together, Little Meerkat, Small Elephant and Mini Monkey had many adventures, which all ended well so long as they worked together – and Little Meerkat took care to stay awake when looking out for danger!

Relaxation ideas from Little Meerkat, Small Elephant and Mini Monkey

I hope you enjoyed this story. In the story, Little Meerkat, Small Elephant and Mini Monkey each had different abilities – sensing danger, understanding and remembering feelings, and solving problems.

Your brain has these abilities, too, and works with your body to help you feel, think, move about and get on with your day.

Your brain has three main parts:

1. **one to look for danger, like Little Meerkat**

2. **another to remember and check how you are feeling, like Small Elephant**

3. **a third part for thinking, working things out, learning and making decisions, as Mini Monkey did in the story.**

Here are a few ideas to help you to feel calmer, just like Mini Monkey!

Think about a place you love to be

It might be on the beach listening to the waves and feeling the sunshine warming your face and body.

Can you shut your eyes for a moment and imagine being in your favourite place?

What can you hear?

What can you see?

What can you feel?

What can you smell?

How do you feel when you are there?

Enjoy being there again, slowly open your eyes and smile as you do. Remember you can visit this place any time you want to feel calm again.

For your body

Try standing on one leg whilst reaching up to the sky.

You might wobble a bit and the Meerkat part of your brain might panic a little! Just feel that big stretch in your arms while you reach them up to the sky, and notice how strong your one leg feels. Now try the other leg and streeetch up again. This will give your Meerkat brain something it likes doing so it can feel calm again.

Breathing it away

You always have your breathing, wherever you go, just like Mini Monkey did when Little Meerkat and Small Monkey were too full of feelings and feeling worried:

Slowly in…and slowly out…

Slowly in…slowly out…

Slowly in…slowly out…

While counting 1234 slowly in…12345678 slowly out

A cooling drink

Often when we get anxious we also get hot! Remember Mini Monkey got everyone to have a cool drink from the water hole before searching for the missing Meerkats? Slow sips can help us when we're anxious, too.

Sharing feelings

Try writing or drawing about your feelings and sharing this with the grown-ups who take care of you so they know what you need. If you are feeling worried or anxious, drawing or writing might be easier than talking about it. With some help to feel calm again, you should soon be able to get on with your day.

My Little Meerkat brain likes singing, dancing, walking, doing yoga, and being gently rocked, stroked, and hugged. We are all different – work out what your Little Meerkat brain likes so it can feel calmer and you can feel more relaxed!

Information for adults

For a wide range of reasons some young children are more anxious than others, and need support to be able to feel calmer and emotionally 'comfortable' enough to enjoy daily life and relationships. I have written this story to help children who are anxious, and have based the characters on the three main areas of the brain, to show what happens when anxiety occurs and how you can use this model with your child to address the anxieties and worries they may have in a simple way.

Introducing the triune brain

Our brains are complicated and amazing things. We are discovering new things about them every day, but there is still a great deal to learn.

American physician and neuroscientist Paul D. MacLean devised the theory of the 'triune brain' back in the 1960s. This theory asserts there are three main areas that work together in our brains: a primitive survival area (the 'reptilian' brain), an emotional memories area (the 'mammalian' or 'limbic' system) and a part for all our intelligent thinking and behaviours (the 'cortex' or 'neocortex'). Information flows between the three areas continuously – unless we are under threat, when the reptilian survival Meerkat brain takes over.

Little Meerkat – the reptilian brain

In the story Little Meerkat represents the primitive *reptilian* brain. This begins forming pre-birth and it is activated automatically if we sense danger or threat. It flicks us into fight, flight and freeze response, preparing our body for action so we stand a chance of surviving.

In the past, daily life was more dangerous and unpredictable. Nowadays, we are more likely to activate our *reptilian* brain if we lose our car keys or are late for work! We panic, can't think straight, our heart beats fast, our breathing becomes shallow and we are at our least intelligent!

This part of our brain is all about surviving from one moment to the next; it is not about thinking or contemplation, as that hesitation could cost us our life...

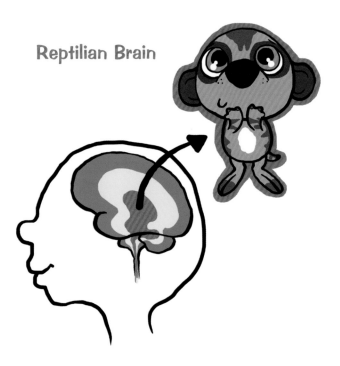

Reptilian Brain

Small Elephant – the limbic system

Small Elephant represents the *limbic* system, where we store and retrieve feelings attached to memories.

The limbic system, sometimes called the 'mammalian brain', is the second part of our brain to grow. It has an important job as it helps us to remember how experiences and people make us feel. When we get very scared by something, this part of our brain will later remember how we felt about it. For example, if you experienced a big storm one day when you were a child, and you felt scared, sad or like running away, but someone you cared about helped you to feel safe again and listened to how you were feeling, the next time a storm happened this part of our brain would have remembered the fear but also the experience that in the end you felt fine again.

In our story, Small Elephant was good at working out feelings and remembering them. Young children benefit greatly when we focus on doing this with them.

For example, 'You can't watch TV right now – that looks like it's hard for you. How are you feeling about it? Sad and angry, big feelings? I am sorry to hear that – would you like a hug or to go and read a book?'

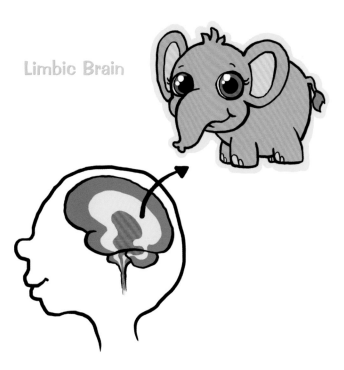

Limbic Brain

Mini Monkey – the cortex

Mini Monkey represents the thinking, intelligent *cortex* part of the brain, which we aim to use most of the time!

It is the third and last part of our brain to fully develop and it helps us to think things through, to be able to plan, wait, learn new things, make and keep relationships, decide what to do when, and be aware of the consequences of our actions. It is less instinctive than the other two parts of the brain and mostly needs to be in charge of them, but not if there is danger or something we need to be afraid of nearby! Then our reptilian survival brain needs to react and act.

Neo-cortex

All three parts of the brain are very important and need to be ready to work together, although threat and danger trigger our survival system and shut off our cortex, as reaction and action trump thinking when we are under threat. The cortex is not fully formed until we are nearly in our 30s.

Example – for an anxious child, any 'big feelings' can overwhelm their system and be perceived as a threat to their safety by their *reptilian* Meerkat brain.

'Busy roads are dangerous and people get knocked down' can trigger a child's anxiety and hence a Meerkat brain type response, where they go into survival mode – can't think, heart is racing and they are flicked into an urge to run, freeze or get angry and upset.

'Roads can be full of cars and lorries so we need to use our clever Monkey brain to help us get across carefully! Breathe deeply, look carefully, listen, look again and if it's clear, over we go.'

How Meerkat, Elephant and Monkey Can Help Children and Adults

The challenge for adults caring for anxious children is to help them develop so they can learn to move from using their Meerkat/*reptilian* brain to their intelligent Monkey/*cortex* brain. Exploring and naming their feelings is key to this process, along with the body-based activities featured at the end of the story.

First, you need to calm the body when it is in 'survival mode' – activities such as breathing, imagining a happy, soothing place or time, stretching and balancing can help, along with being aware of how this feels in the body.

Remember, young children are mostly operating in Meerkat and Elephant brain modes, full of feelings, easily overwhelmed with little ability to rationalise and calm themselves down. The more they are soothed and calmed and can learn with you ways to do these as they develop, the less likely they are to panic and experience long-term stress and anxiety.

This book is for children, but it's also important for us as adults to think about our Meerkat, Elephant and Monkey brains. The more we take care of our own Meerkat brain, reduce our anxiety and use 'feelings-first' approach, the more relaxed our children will be!